THE ADVENTURES OF

Izzy and Columbus

NAKAMOMO ISLAND

The Adventures of Izzy and Columbus - Nakamomo Island

Published by The Conrad Press in the United Kingdom 2020

Tel: +44(0)1227 472 874
www.theconradpress.com
info@theconradpress.com

ISBN 978-1-911546-77-1

Illustrations by Marta Maszkiewicz

Typesetting by: Charlotte Mouncey, www.bookstyle.co.uk

The Conrad Press logo was designed by Maria Priestley.

Printed and bound in Great Britain by Clays Ltd, Elcograf S.p.A.

BOOK ONE

OF THE ADVENTURES OF
Izzy and Columbus

SERIES

THE ADVENTURES OF

Izzy and Columbus

NAKAMOMO ISLAND

Zoe Verner

Illustrations by Marta Maszkiewicz

This book is dedicated with love
to Zac Dylan Pitt

CHAPTER ONE

The break in

The weekend had arrived in sunny London and all the kids of Gibbons Road were outside playing. It was a no-exit road, the ideal spot for them all to get together. Izzy had her play clothes on, a bright red t-shirt with blue denim jeans. She rarely wore dresses, unless her mum made her put one on for a special occasion.

Izzy was jumping up and down with excitement, 'Let the adventures begin!' she shouted to her dog Columbus as she threw his favourite red ball for him. 'Go get it, Columbus!'

Columbus pounced to catch the ball and brought it back to Izzy, covered in his slimy slobber, she was used to this but it always made her giggle. When she threw the ball again, she accidentally tripped on her shoelace and threw it into her neighbour's house, Mr. Niri. He had left a window wide open and the ball had gone straight through!

All the kids gasped in horror.

The street fell silent.

Mr. Niri lived alone and rarely left his house. He was a strange man who kept to himself. He was tall with jet-black hair and a pale face. On the rare occasions he was out walking around, he always kept his head hung low, so no one could quite see his face. Nobody on the street knew much about him, they all called him 'Eerie Niri'. He would never say 'hello' to anyone.

He owned two cats called Boris and Doris. One was ginger and one was black, they each wore bright red collars and would sit on the steps of his house and hiss at anyone who walked by. Every few hours Mr. Niri would come out, give them some milk, take a furtive look up and down the street, give them a stroke each and then go back inside. No one had ever seen the inside of his house. One of Izzy's neighbours, Maisie McKelling, had told everyone that she had once seen through his window and caught Mr. Niri drinking a huge glass of thick, red blood! This soon led to a rumour that he was a blood-drinking vampire, and would roam the streets at night searching for new victims.

Izzy had just turned nine years old. She lived with her Mum, Dad, big brother Zac and their dog, Columbus. She had a very captivating face with tiny freckles sprinkled over her cheeks. Her eyes were a striking emerald green and she always wore her long, brown hair in a messy plat. Izzy was extremely intelligent for her age, she was top of the class in Maths and had also won the School Chess Championship three years in a row.

Columbus was a gorgeous fox-red Labrador with a teddy bear face. He was a present for her sixth birthday. He was just a tiny puppy back then and Izzy immediately fell in love with him, he soon became her best friend. They went everywhere together; to the park, to the shops, to the library, she even took him to her school. The teachers didn't mind as they all adored him and he helped out at lunch time by gobbling up any leftover food. Izzy would often pretend they were going on a big expedition, she would draw maps and make up imaginary places, even if they were just going to the shops and back it was always an adventure. At night Columbus curled up and slept at the end of her bed. They were never apart.

One of Izzy's best friends on the street was called Max. He was also in her class at school. He had a cheeky, round face, ginger spiky hair, and was always getting into trouble with his teachers.

He was known at school for being extremely naughty, his nickname was 'Mental Max'. Not many kids were allowed to play with him, but Izzy and her family adored him. Max had seen the ball fly into Mr. Niri's house and ran over to Izzy.

'Oh no! Izz, that's Eerie Niri's house! What are you going to do?' he asked with a look of mischief on his face.

'Out of all the windows on the street, why this one!' said Izzy stamping her foot. 'Columbus has loved that ball since he was a puppy. I bet Mr. Niri would never give it back to me. I'm far too scared to ask him! What can I do Max?'

Max looked at Columbus's sad face. 'Right Izz, there's only one thing for it… we've got to go in and get it back!'

Izzy looked worried. 'Are you crazy? Max, this is Eerie Niri we are talking about. What if he catches us and then drinks our blood or even worse!?'

'I'm not scared of him,' Max replied, with his head held high. 'Don't worry, I'll protect us. We need to get the ball back, for Columbus.' Columbus jumped up with excitement and licked Max on his face

Izzy smiled. 'OK Max. Let's do it! But we need a plan.'

Suddenly, Izzy's mum popped her head out of the front door.

'Izzy Whizzy!' she shouted, almost singing her name. 'Tea and cake time! Oh, hello, Max, would you like some too?'

Max looked up with a huge smile on his face. 'Yes please!' he shouted back. 'Izz, let's go in and have some of your mum's awesome cakes while we form a plan.'

Izzy's mum's cakes were famous on the street. You could smell the magical scent of vanilla and chocolate wafting out of her kitchen. Izzy always knew when her mum was baking, as she would sing her cake song:

'All things sweet, all things yummy, cakes and treats made by mummy.'

They all ran to Izzy's house where she had set up tea and cake in the garden. Izzy's family had a beautiful garden, lots of brightly coloured flowers, and a big pond full of fish. Izzy and Max sat round the garden table enjoying the scrummy cakes while Columbus chewed on a big bone.

Max, stuffing his face with cake, said, 'Right… Mr. Niri always goes out at lunch time. I don't know where he goes but it's always the same time.'

'I heard he goes looking for victims.' Izzy said, nervously sipping her tea.

'Or maybe he has to attend some sort of vampire meeting,' Max replied. 'I think we should wait until he leaves and then sneak in through the open window.'

'The window it is. But what about Boris and Doris?'

Boris and Doris weren't like normal cats. They did not chase mice or run around playing, and they did not curl up and sleep. They were constantly on guard and never left Mr. Niri's steps.

'Columbus could scare them off!' suggested Izzy.

'But, Columbus isn't scary!' Max objected.

'He can be,' said Izzy. 'Columbus, show Max your scariest face.'

Columbus jumped up and gave them a snarl, showing

off all his lovely white teeth.

Max laughed. 'Oh, Columbus, you could never look scary to me, but I think that might just work. We should all go inside together, that way Columbus can sniff out his ball while we keep watch.'

Izzy agreed, 'OK cool. I can't wait to see what Eerie Niri's house looks like inside!'

'Me too!' said Max. 'Once Columbus has scared off Boris and Doris, I'll give you a leg up through the window, then you can pull me in, and Columbus can jump in after us. He'll find his ball, and we can quickly escape through the front door. The street is usually pretty quiet at lunch time, as everyone is inside eating, so hopefully no one will see us sneak in and out.'

Once they had finished their tea and cake, they jumped up and headed back onto the street. It was time to put their plan into action!

Boris and Doris were sitting on Mr. Niri's steps as usual, guarding his house like two soldiers, looking up and down the street.

'Right Columbus,' said Max, 'it's time for you to get scary. Run up to Boris and Doris and growl like you've never growled before.'

Columbus nodded his head and shot off. He bounded up the steps towards the two cats with a menacing growl bearing all his teeth.

Boris and Doris arched their backs and hissed at

Columbus. They stayed put on the steps. Columbus growled even louder, but again no luck.

'OK,' said Max, 'time for plan number two.'

Before Izzy had a chance to ask what plan number two was, Max was off. He started running as fast as he could towards the cats, screeching and wildly waving his arms around in the air. The cats looked at Max in terror as he ran closer and closer towards them, loudly screaming his head off. They puffed up their fur and tails, jumped off the steps, and bolted!

'Yes!' shouted Izzy, triumphantly clapping her hands. 'Nice one Max, it worked!'

'Well Izz, they don't call me 'Mental Max' for nothing,' Max laughed. 'Right, now we have to get you through that window! There's no time to waste!'

They ran up to the house. Max lifted Izzy up to the window, she wobbled a little bit but then managed to grab onto the window ledge. She pulled herself up and jumped inside. Little did Izzy know, that after jumping through that window, everything was about to change.

CHAPTER TWO

The mysterious map

Izzy had landed in Mr. Niri's study with a bump. She quickly got up and helped pull Max in. He came flying through the window and went head first into Mr. Niri's desk! A moment later Columbus jumped through and landed right on top of Max. Izzy could not stop laughing, but it soon dawned on her that they had broken into Mr. Niri's house, and if anyone found out they would all be in serious trouble.

'Max, Columbus, are you both OK?' Izzy asked. 'That was some crazy entrance!'

Max, who was a little dazed, scrambled to his feet.

'That was cool!' he said, rubbing his head. He looked

around. 'Wow! I can't believe we are actually inside Erie Niri's house! Hmm, it looks pretty normal for a vampire's house.'

The study was huge with tons of books piled up everywhere, and there was a huge map on the wall.

'Max, we must be super quiet,' Izzy warned. 'No one can know we're here. We don't have much time. Columbus, quickly go find your ball.'

Columbus went straight to the back of the room where there was a large, dark red, velvet curtain. Max looked at Izzy with a mischievous grin. He headed over to the curtain and pulled it back. Before they could see what was behind it, Columbus darted forward and sniffed out his ball. The curtain revealed even more books, a giant wooden chest, and a huge map rolled up and tied with a gold ribbon. Izzy curiously picked up the map and untied the bow. At the top of the map was a strange name.

'Nakamomo Island,' she read aloud. 'I've never heard of that before, have you Max?'

'Nope, but I'm not very good at geography. Just ask Mrs. Ford!'

They both laughed.

'Well, you know how much I love geography, I'm pretty sure this island doesn't exist.'

Max headed over to the wooden chest. It was beautiful with all different kinds of animals carved into the sides. The lid was covered with bright, twinkly, gemstones.

'I wonder what's inside?' Max asked eagerly.

'This is wrong,' Izzy replied, whist rolling the map back up. 'We shouldn't even be in here, and now we are going through Mr. Niri's personal belongings.'

'Oh, don't be boring, a quick look won't hurt... '

Suddenly, Columbus came running in, his eyes wide with alarm. Izzy instantly knew what this meant. She threw the map over to Max, and ran over to the window.

'Oh, no! Mr. Niri's coming back!' she said frantically. 'What shall we do Max?'

'Guys, get in the chest!' Max cried in a panic.

They heard the front door open.

Izzy picked up Columbus, and they both jumped inside the chest just as Mr. Niri was approaching the room. With the map still grasped tightly in his hand, Max jumped in last. The lid slammed shut and they were plunged into darkness.

The chest started to shake!

They were all falling... falling... falling... and then without warning, they landed with an almighty thud.

Izzy opened her eyes and was blinded by sunlight. She wiped palm leaves from her face and looked around. She couldn't believe her eyes. She was no longer inside Mr. Niri's chest, she wasn't even in Mr. Niri's house, and she certainly wasn't on Gibbons Road anymore. She was surrounded by trees, and could hear the sounds of exotic birds. She was getting hotter and hotter by the minute...

Izzy was in the middle of a tropical rainforest!

She was in total shock. Was this a dream? Had she banged her head? It took her a while to try and understand what had just happened. One minute she had been jumping into Mr. Niri's chest, and now she's standing in the middle of a jungle! The rainforest was beautiful, dominated by magnificent tall trees letting in tiny glimpses of glittering sunlight. The trees looked almost human with huge vein-like roots going into the ground. All of a sudden, she felt a wet nose push against her cheek.

'Columbus! You're here! Boy am I glad to see you!'

She cuddled him tightly and showered him in kisses. They both looked around for Max, but he was nowhere to be seen.

'It must be some kind of magical portal. Remember that map? It said 'Nakamomo Island' do you think that's where we are, Columbus?' Izzy asked, as she looked around more confused than ever. 'Where on earth could Max be… ?'

Suddenly out of nowhere, she heard a kind, strangely familiar sounding voice. It was a very young and playful boy's voice.

'Maybe Max got lost on the way here, Izzy; remember he was the last one to jump into the chest… '

Izzy froze. Who could that be? She thought. Somehow, she knew that voice, but it could not be… it just could not. She turned around and there was Columbus. 'Izzy, it's me. I can talk!'

Izzy's eyes and mouth grew wider and wider. 'Columbus!' Izzy yelled in shock. 'Wow, you can talk! You can really talk! This is amazing!'

Columbus spun around in excitement. 'I've always wanted to talk to you Izzy!'

Izzy was stunned. She had first been transported from her street to a tropical jungle, and now Columbus was talking! She just couldn't believe what she was hearing. Columbus was *talking* to her.

'Columbus this is incredible! Talk more, talk more!'

Columbus laughed, 'This feels really weird. It's like a dream. Tell me it's real, it's real isn't it, Izzy?'

'Yes, Columbus this is really happening. Now, we must try and find Max. I don't know which way to go, if only we had that map.'

'Look Izzy!' said Columbus, lifting his paw. 'A banana tree!'

'Oh, how cool! I'm super hungry, let's pick some. I know how much you love bananas.'

The bananas were a vibrant yellow colour. Izzy jumped up and broke two off. No sooner had she done so than a small monkey appeared.

'Excuse me,' said the monkey sternly, in a very posh voice, 'but those are my bananas.'

Izzy jumped back and dropped the bananas. She stared at the monkey in astonishment.

'It's rude to stare,' said the monkey, 'and it's very rude to take things without asking!'

He was a capuchin monkey with a cute, white, fluffy face, and a dark brown fury body. He was wearing a little red bow tie. He had a superior manner about him.

Izzy kindly tried to apologise to the monkey, 'I'm terribly sorry, I just didn't know they were yours. The thing is, er, Mr. Monkey, my dog, Columbus, absolutely loves bananas and I'm starving.'

'It's polite to call somebody by their correct name. My name is Martin!' snapped the monkey in a very well-spoken tone. 'You may have one banana each.'

'Thank you, Martin,' said Columbus.

'Yes, thank you, Martin,' Izzy added gratefully. 'That's very kind of you. I'm sorry but I've never met a talking monkey before.'

Martin looked at Izzy curiously, and then enquired, 'Where exactly are you both from?'

'We're from London,' Izzy replied.

Martin looked puzzled. 'London?' he said. 'I haven't heard of London before. Which island is that?'

Izzy giggled. 'It's on a gigantic Island, it's called Great Britain.'

Martin looked even more confused. 'No. It doesn't ring a bell I'm afraid. How did you get here?'

'Well, it's all very strange,' Izzy began to explain, 'Columbus and I, and my friend Max, were hiding in my neighbour's chest. It was a sort of treasure chest, and then the next thing we knew was we were all falling through darkness, and then Columbus and I landed here. Max is nowhere to be seen.'

'Hmm,' said Martin tapping his fury hand on his chin. 'That is extremely strange indeed. I have heard about this chest before. Who is your neighbour?'

'His name is Mr. Niri,' answered Izzy.

Martin looked shocked.

'Do you know him?' she asked.

Martin began to tell Izzy all about how Mr. Niri used to live on Nakamomo Island a long time ago, 'Mr. Niri was banished by the king of the island but I don't know what happened, or what he did to make the king so angry.'

'Was it because they found out he was a vampire?' asked Izzy

Martin laughed, 'A vampire?' he said with amusement. 'He is not a vampire, they don't exist. Why on earth would you think that?'

'Well I dunno, he's a very odd man. A girl who lives on our street said she once saw him drink blood!' Izzy explained, trying to convince Martin it was true.

Martin smiled. 'That's the most ridiculous thing I've ever heard. Young children love to spread rumours. I don't know this Mr. Niri well, but I'm certain he is not a vampire.'

'OK, you're right, it is a bit ridiculous,' Izzy agreed, feeling a little silly. 'Well, he must have done something really bad to never to be allowed back. I wonder what it was…'

It was getting dark in the rainforest. Izzy, Columbus

and Martin, were looking for a big tree for them to climb up, with a branch strong enough to sleep on.

'How about that one, Martin?' asked Columbus pointing his paw at a tree.

'No,' replied Martin firmly. 'That one hasn't got enough branches. You don't want to fall off in the middle of the night, do you Columbus?'

Izzy looked at Columbus and quietly giggled.

'I will take you all to one of my favourite sleeping spots!' Martin called out as he swung up into the branches. 'Follow me, if you can keep up!'

Martin swung from tree to tree leading the way, his tail curling up as he whizzed through the air. Izzy and Columbus ran behind him, trying hard not to be distracted by their new and exciting surroundings. They ran passed trees covered in huge green vines and brightly coloured exotic plants. They could hear many strange and wonderful sounds coming from amongst the tall green palms. Martin had slowed down and was hanging off a tree branch waiting for them. As they drew closer to him the sound of gushing water came to their ears. There was a magnificent waterfall behind the tree that Martin was on.

Izzy gasped. 'Oh Martin, this is one of the coolest things I have ever seen!'

Columbus ran up to the waterfall and yelled out, 'Wow, I can see loads of fish in the water!'

'Columbus, those fish are not for eating,' warned Martin. Izzy laughed.

Columbus looked disappointed. 'OK, Martin, I'll be good,' he promised.

Martin jumped off the tree onto a rock and pointed to a humongous tree further up by the waterfall. Izzy had never seen a tree so tall and majestic.

'This is a Kapok tree,' Martin announced. 'It's one of the tallest trees in the rainforest. This is where we will sleep tonight.'

'Awesome!' Izzy exclaimed, as she gazed up. The trunk was bigger than Izzy's house. The branches were a radiant, luscious green. Hidden within the branches were a small group of toucans. They all seemed to be staring at Izzy and whispering.

Columbus bounded up the tree to the first branch. 'Now this is my kind of tree.'

Martin reached down and lifted Izzy up onto the first branch.

'Thank you Martin, you are a real gentleman.'

Martin smiled. 'Always a pleasure,' he said, as he dipped down his furry head in a little bow.

They all slowly climbed further up the tree until they reached a huge branch that looked strong enough to support them all.

'This one looks good,' Izzy said, as she jumped onto it testing its strength.

'Oh yes,' agreed Martin. 'This one will do nicely.'

Izzy curled up with Columbus as the sun began to set. The view was breath-taking. Beautiful shades of pink and orange filled the sky and small droplets of water from the waterfall were bouncing off the tree.

Martin found a nice spot at the end of the branch and dangled his little legs over the edge.

'Ahhhhh...' he yawned. 'This is very comfy. Good night Izzy, good night Columbus. Sleep well chaps.'

'Good night Martin,' said Izzy, as her eyes began to close. 'See you in the morning, and thank you for looking after us.'

Martin gave Izzy a little nod as he drifted off to sleep.

'Columbus,' Izzy whispered. 'I'm so worried about Max. I hope he has found somewhere nice to sleep. I hate not knowing where he is. What if he's in danger or injured?!'

Columbus licked Izzy's cheek. 'Don't worry Izz, Max is tough. I'm sure he's absolutely fine and probably fast asleep right now somewhere very safe. We will find him soon and be home in no time, and then we can tell everyone back home all about our adventure.'

Izzy smiled. 'Yeah, Zac is going to be soooooo jealous.'

They all fell asleep peacefully under the stars.

CHAPTER THREE

Flying to Wendy's house

A new day dawned in the rainforest. Sun beams were warming up Izzy's cheeks and she had her own personal choir of pretty birds singing to her from the branch above. Izzy was the first to wake up. She had completely forgotten where she was and when she reached out to turn on her bedside light, like she does every morning, she almost fell off the branch. As she shook her head and opened her eyes she remembered what had happened and looked around her. The refreshing morning mist was rising over the tropical jungle, it was warm and damp. The smell of the jungle was incredible. She felt alive and excited for what the new day would bring. She was feeling positive that they would soon find Max and he would be telling her all about what he'd been up to. Whilst she was gazing at her surroundings a brightly coloured toucan flew up and perched on the branch next to her.

'Good morning there Missy,' said the toucan, with a friendly smile. He had a huge bright green and orange beak with a purple tip. His body was a silky black and his face a striking yellow.

'Oh gosh, you shocked me!' said Izzy as she widened her eyes and took in all the gorgeous colours of the toucan. 'You are beautiful,' she exclaimed in amazement.

'Why thank you. How kind,' the toucan replied.

'My name's Izzy, what's yours?' she asked him.

The toucan flew up right next to her and said: 'My name is Alex, I'm a sailor.'

Izzy smiled. 'Cool! I've never met a sailor before. Do you have a boat then?'

'Yes, of course I have a boat. What kind of sailor would I be without a boat?' he laughed. 'It's moored up on the beach. Do you wanna see it?'

Izzy's whole face lit up. 'Oh yeah, I'd love that.'

'We don't see many young girls in the jungle,' said the toucan. 'What are you doing here?'

Izzy explained her story to Alex, 'So you see, now we are stuck here and we need to find Max,' she finished. Alex looked concerned, 'You say you jumped into Mr.

Niri's chest?'

'Yes, that's right,' Izzy confirmed. 'Have you heard of him?'

Alex fluffed his feathers and began to tell Izzy how he had met Mr. Niri once…

'There was a big wedding in town. The king's daughter, Madison, was getting married to a man called Logan. He was a dashing young man who came from a very wealthy and important family. Everybody had been talking about it for months. During the ceremony the guests were asked if anyone had any reason why they should not be wed. Surprisingly Mr. Niri stood up, in-front of everyone, and confessed his love for Madison.'

'Really?' said Izzy in shock. 'I can't imagine Mr. Niri doing something like that. What happened next?'

Alex continued, 'Turns out they had been secretly in love for years.

Poor Mr. Niri couldn't watch her marry the wrong man without saying something. It was all very dramatic. The next thing we knew; Madison ran out of the chapel with Mr. Niri, leaving Logan standing at the altar. It must have been very embarrassing for him. All I know now is that Madison's father, the king, was furious with Mr. Niri. He sent his soldiers to track them down and forced her to marry Logan. Madison now lives with Logan at the palace.'

'That's such an upsetting story,' Izzy said. 'It explains

why Mr. Niri is so lonely and keeps to himself. I was always really scared of him, but he sounds like a really sweet person. I feel sorry for him.'

'Yes, me too,' agreed Alex the toucan. 'I do believe she loved Mr. Niri very much. It's so unfair how he was treated.'

'It's all terribly sad,' Martin sighed, who had been listening with Columbus from the other branch.

'So that must be why the king banished him from this special place,' said Columbus as he stretched out his fury paws on the branch.

'The king is known for having quite a temper!' added Martin.

Izzy's eyes opened wide, 'I've got it!' she said. 'We must go and see the king! He is the only person that can help us. Surely he will know where Max is.'

'He knows everything,' Alex agreed. 'Nothing escapes his radar. He is not a nice man though so you will need your wits about you.'

'I don't care, I just need to find Max,' Izzy said with a determined face.

'I understand, it's so awful, that you have lost your friend. We must get to my boat so I can take you to the king.'

Izzy introduced Alex to Columbus and Martin and filled them in on her plan to see the king.

'Oh, how fabulous,' said Martin, as he shook Alex's wing. 'I absolutely love the ocean - and how very kind of you Alex for helping us.'

Columbus stretched out and smiled. 'Yay Izzy, when we get to the sea I can have a nice swim.'

Izzy laughed, 'Columbus loves swimming.'

Alex looked pleased. 'Well then, let's get going! It will take us at least a day to get to the coast. We can stop off at Wendy's house on the way. She's such a lovely lady and we can spend the night at her home by the river. Wendy is one of the best cooks I've ever met and she makes incredible chocolate, fresh from her coco bean farm. Oh, and her banana bread is famous on the island – you're all going to love it there.'

'How exciting!' said Izzy, 'Wendy sounds so cool, I can't wait to meet her. Thanks Alex.'

Martin licked his lips. 'I absolutely adore banana bread, this is a marvellous idea, count me in!'

They all jumped down from the Kapok tree and started to follow Alex through the rainforest.

'Izzy!' shouted Alex. 'Why don't you hop on my back for a bit and check out the view!'

Izzy needed no convincing, she smiled and instantly jumped up onto Alex's fluffy back. 'This is so comfy Alex,' she said as she felt his smooth feathers with her hands.

Alex rose up, soaring through the tall trees.

'Wow! This is so incredible!' she shouted with the fresh wind in her face and her plat whipping around in the air.

Columbus picked up the pace to keep up with them

as Martin swung above him from tree to tree yelling out, 'Let's go! Wahoooooooo!'

⟨ornament⟩

They had all been travelling to Wendy's for several hours now and were beginning to get very hot, tired, and hungry.

'Look guys!' Izzy shouted. 'There's a river ahead!'

Columbus saw the river and suddenly bounded off. 'Yahoooo!' he yelled. 'I'm so hot I'm going to dive straight in.'

Izzy laughed, 'Me too. Let's all jump in!'

They all headed towards the river.

'Thank you, sailor Alex,' Izzy said jumping off his back. 'That was some ride!'

Columbus was the first in. He swam around with a huge smile on his face. Then Izzy and Martin both jumped in too.

'Oh, this is fabulous,' said Martin, as he bobbed along with his head held high.

'Look!' shouted Alex, pointing to a pretty house on the other side of the river. 'That's Wendy's house.'

'Wonderful!' said Martin.

'It looks so homely and inviting,' Izzy said smiling. 'Alex, are you sure Wendy won't mind us spending the night?'

'Of course not, she gets lonely sometimes, and absolutely loves visitors. She will be so happy to see us.'

Wendy's house was all made out of wood and surrounding

it were lots of big banana trees with hammocks tied up between them. They walked up to a large porch area and as Izzy was about to knock on the door, it opened and she heard a loud: 'Helloooooooo, I saw you all walking up to the house from the window. Welcome, welcome. Come in, come in. I'm Wendy.'

Wendy had an extremely friendly face, very tanned and pretty with big rosy cheeks covered in freckles. Her hair was short, dark and curly and she had the most beautiful big smile. She was wearing a green dress with a bright red polka dot apron. Alex flew in and landed on Wendy's shoulder.

'Hello my lovely Wendy!' he said, as he rubbed his beak against her cheek. 'This is my new friend Izzy and her dog Columbus. And this little monkey is Martin.'

Wendy grabbed Alex and gave him a huge squeeze. 'Hello dearest Alex. Oh, I have missed you! And a big welcome to Izzy, Martin, and Columbus.'

Wendy ushered everyone into her home.

'Right! First thing's first. Let's get you all some food,' she said.

Columbus's ears pricked up, 'Yes please!'

She showed everyone out onto the garden terrace at the back of the house. There was a big, wooden dining table and an outside kitchen area.

'Help yourselves to my homemade lemonade - it's there on the table. I will start bringing the food out. I hope you're all super hungry.'

Everyone replied with big grins, 'Yes we are!'

Wendy headed into the outside kitchen and started busying herself with pots and pans.

'Right, Alex,' said Izzy, as she slurped her ice-cold lemonade, 'what's the plan for tomorrow?'

'The coast is only a few hours from here, so I think we should get up nice and early and head to my boat.'

'OK, wicked.' Izzy said excitedly.

Wendy overheard in the kitchen and said, 'It sounds like you'll have a big day ahead of you and breakfast is the most important meal of the day. I'll prepare you all one of my special breakfasts in the morning before you go.'

'Thanks Wendy, that sounds perfect,' said Izzy.

Alex agreed, 'Wendy's breakfasts are the best in the whole jungle.'

Wendy smiled and looked proud. She finished cooking in the kitchen and started bringing out her special dinner - well it was more like a feast.

'Dinner is served!' she announced.

Wendy had cooked a huge plate of grilled chicken, stewed black beans, fried plantains, a big bowl of rice and, as if that wasn't enough, a giant red snapper fish! Everyone's jaws were on the floor as she kept bringing out more and more food. Martin started clapping, and then everyone else joined in.

'Oh, Wendy, this looks like a dream,' Izzy said, with a

huge grin. 'I wish Max was here to meet you, he is the biggest pig I know. He would love this meal.'

Wendy sat down at the table and told them all to dig in. Once everyone started helping themselves to the delicious spread Wendy asked Izzy how she had arrived in the jungle and what had happened to her friend Max. Izzy told her all about Mr. Niri and the chest, and the crazy adventure that had followed. Wendy was shocked and gave Izzy a huge cuddle, 'That's some story! I have actually known Mr. Niri for a long time,' Wendy told them.

Everyone at the table looked at her, intrigued to know more.

'You know Mr. Niri?' Izzy asked, immediately bursting with questions.

'Yes, ever since he was a little boy,' Wendy explained. 'It's terrible that he was banished for falling in love.'

Izzy was eager to know more and so Wendy began to tell them all about Mr. Niri and Madison.

'Mr. Niri, well I know him as James, grew up with his family just down the river from here. He used to play in my garden. There weren't many kids here for him to play with. I was worried that he might get a bit bored so whenever I had the time I would try and play with him. We created some great games together.'

Wendy looked wistful and began chuckling to herself.

'I taught him how to make chocolate. He was so keen to learn all about my farm. Such a cute boy... His parents were away a lot so he used to stay here with me. He was on his own so much I felt sorry for him. Most nights he would fall asleep in one of my hammocks. As he grew older he started working on the farm, and he stood out from all the others. He was the first one at work in the morning and the last to leave at night. Out of everyone he worked the hardest. I'd cook him dinner and we'd talk for hours under the stars. One day there was a knock at the door... '

Everyone moved closer to Wendy, hanging on every word she was saying.

'It was the king's guardsmen recruiting young men to go and work for the king. I told them all about James and they seemed very impressed. I called him into the house so he could meet them and, before I knew it, he had packed his bags and he was ready to go! I'd never seen him so excited.'

Wendy smiled at their attentive faces.

'He sent me lots of letters. I had one each week,' she continued. 'He told me how much he was enjoying working for the king and that he had fallen in love with a girl. He didn't tell me who she was at first, but then eventually he told me she was the king's daughter, Madison. Then one day they both came to visit me. Madison was a lovely girl, very beautiful and kind. Anyone could see they were completely in love, but they asked me not to tell anyone as it was all a secret. Madison told me about how the king had arranged for her to marry Logan and that she didn't want to - she wanted to be with James.'

Izzy looked deeply upset, 'Why couldn't they just tell the king that they were in love?'

'That's what I asked them, Izzy,' Wendy answered. 'Madison explained that her father wouldn't approve. James wasn't from a royal family and she didn't want him to get fired, or worse.'

'That's so unfair,' said Izzy. 'When you love someone, it shouldn't matter what family they are from or how much money they have.'

'That is very sad indeed,' agreed Martin. 'I can see now why they had to run away together.'

'It was the only way they could be together,' said Izzy, yawning and stretching her arms out.

Everyone else around the table started to yawn too.

'Oh, look at you all, you must be so tired after your journey here,' Wendy exclaimed, clearing the table. 'Right! Hot chocolate time, then off to bed!'

Wendy stroked Columbus on the head. 'Now Columbus, you can't eat chocolate, so I have some yummy doggy biscuits for you.'

'Thanks, Wendy!' said Columbus, licking his lips.

Everyone else waited eagerly to try Wendy's famous chocolate.

Martin was very excited - he had been telling Izzy all about how much he loved hot chocolate. 'I do try and watch my weight,' he said. 'I eat very well in the jungle, but I can't resist a cheeky hot chocolate!'

'Oh, me too Martin,' admitted Izzy with a cheeky smile.

'Just wait until you try Wendy's,' said Alex. 'It's the best chocolate I have ever had.'

Wendy brought out a huge wooden bowl filled to the brim with her delicious hot chocolate. 'It's chocolate time!'

She put the bowl in the middle of the table. Then, using a huge ladle, poured everyone a cup of hot chocolate. She gave Columbus his doggy treats, which he gobbled up immediately.

'Wendy that smells incredible,' said Martin almost falling off his chair as he grabbed a cup. He took a sip, 'I'm in chocolate heaven. It's so smooth and rich and just the right amount of sweetness.'

Izzy nodded as she took a huge gulp.

Alex laughed, 'I told you all, Wendy's is the best.'

Izzy asked if Wendy knew what had happened to Mr. Niri and Madison, 'Where did they run away to?' she asked, whilst enjoying her hot chocolate.

Wendy replied, 'They both came back here. They didn't think the king would find them here, but he has eyes and ears everywhere, and a few days later his guards came knocking on my door looking for them.'

Martin gasped and asked Wendy, 'What did you do?'

'I tried to deny that they were here, but they insisted

on searching the house and they found them. It was just awful - there was nothing I could do.'

'How terrible,' said Izzy. 'What did the king do to them?'

'He sent Madison back to the palace and made her marry Logan and he banished James. He said James was never to return here and he was never to see Madison ever again.'

Izzy looked down at the table with sadness, 'That's just not right.'

Wendy sighed, 'I know, it's very unfair.'

Martin then yawned very loudly and everyone turned to look at him.

'Oh, dear me,' he said, looking embarrassed. 'I'm so sorry.'

Everyone laughed. Wendy stood up and cleared the rest of the table.

'Where would you all like to sleep?' she asked. 'You can sleep in the house, I can make up some beds or you can sleep in the hammocks outside?'

'Hmmmm,' said Izzy dreamily, looking at the sky. 'It's such a hot and beautiful evening I'd like to sleep in a hammock. Columbus you can sleep with me too!'

Alex and Martin agreed they would like to sleep outside too.

Columbus jumped onto Izzy's lap and wagged his tail.

'Good choice,' said Wendy. 'It's a gorgeous evening, you can see the stars so clearly tonight.'

They all gave Wendy a good night hug and thanked her

for the fantastic meal. She took them to the porch and they chose their favourite hammock. Izzy jumped into the biggest one as she was sharing with Columbus.

'It's so comfy!' she said, as Columbus jumped up.

'Oh yes,' Martin agreed. 'This will do nicely.'

Alex was swinging from side to side, 'It's so much fun!'

'It's very relaxing,' said Izzy, as she gazed up at the stars. 'I feel so peaceful here.'

'Good night all. What a stupendous day it's been,' said Martin as he curled his tail around himself.

Izzy smiled at Martin, 'It's been a day I'll never forget,' she said. 'I just wish Max was here to have experienced it with us. I hope he's safe, wherever he is.'

'Don't worry Izzy,' said Alex. 'Tomorrow we will sail my boat to the king's palace and we will find your friend. I promise everything will be alright.'

'Thanks Alex. Good night everyone.'

CHAPTER FOUR

An unexpected guest

The bright orange sun was rising over the river and birds were tweeting as Wendy prepared breakfast in the kitchen.

'Good morning my lovelies!' she shouted whilst pulling out a loaf of freshly baked banana bread from the oven. 'Rise and shine. You have a big day ahead of you. Breakfast is ready!'

Izzy opened her eyes and blinked in the sunlight as Columbus stretched out his arms and gave her a big lick on her face. She giggled, 'Good morning gorgeous Columbus. Good morning everyone! Breakfast smells incredible Wendy.'

Alex started swinging in his hammock, 'Good morning all! I had such a great sleep - I definitely need to get one of these hammocks for my boat.'

Martin let out a big yawn and smiled, 'Oh, I had a fabulous sleep too! I was worried I might have fallen out in the middle of the night as it was my first time sleeping in a hammock, but I slept like a baby.'

Everyone was laughing as they all jumped up and headed to the kitchen where Wendy had sliced up the loaf and put it in the middle of the table.

'Banana bread!' yelled Martin with excitement. 'My absolute favourite.'

Wendy laughed, 'It's my favourite too. Help yourself to fresh coconut water, I picked the coconuts off the tree this morning, just grab a straw.'

They all sat at the table and got stuck in. Izzy took a huge slice of the bread and popped a straw into one of the coconuts. The banana bread was lovely and warm from the oven and the coconut water was cool and refreshing.

'This is the nicest breakfast ever,' said Izzy going back for seconds. Martin nodded frantically, his mouth completely full.

Alex agreed. 'It's just what we need before our big day. I can't wait to show you all my boat, the weather today is perfect for sailing.'

Everyone had lots of questions about their adventure

ahead. Alex explained to them it would take around five hours to get to the coast from Wendy's house. Suddenly Wendy had a great idea…

'Why don't you all take my canoe? It's a big one so you'll all fit nicely. You can paddle down the river until you reach the sea. It should only take a few hours.' Martin leapt up out of his seat, 'That sounds splendid.'

Alex agreed, 'Yes that will be much easier, we'll get to my boat in no time.'

Izzy gave Wendy a huge hug, 'Thank you Wendy that's so kind of you. Let's get going soon guys, the faster we get to Alex's boat the faster we can reach the palace and find Max.'

◊

Wendy had baked some treats for their journey and packed lots of fresh coconuts. She handed Izzy the bag, 'Stay safe my darling girl, I really hope you find your friend, Max. This is not goodbye, something tells me I will be seeing you again.'

Izzy gave Wendy a kiss on the cheek, 'You're such a special person, I think I will be seeing you again too.' She turned to the others, 'Right gang, is everyone ready?'

'Yep!' they all replied with excited smiles.

'To the canoe!' said Martin as he led the way.

◊

Shortly after they left, there was a knock at Wendy's door…

'Oh dear,' she said to herself as she approached the door, 'did you guys forget something?'

She opened the door... It was not Izzy and the gang, as she had expected, but another familiar face. It was Mr. Niri.

'Hello lovely Wendy,' he greeted giving her a big hug. 'It's been far too long.'

'My dearest James, it's so lovely to see you! Yes, it's been almost two years! Come in, come in.'

James sat down in the kitchen, 'Can I please have some of your wonderful hot chocolate?' he asked.

'Coming right up!'

Wendy poured the chocolate into his old mug and passed it to him.

James took a sip, 'This brings back memories.'

Wendy told James how she'd met Izzy and Columbus and how Max had got lost.

'It's all my fault,' James admitted as he sipped his hot chocolate. 'I should have hidden that wooden chest better. I just never thought they would dare enter my house! Before I had a chance to stop him, I saw Max jump into the chest holding one of my maps. That's how they got here and that's how he's been split up from Izzy and Columbus.'

'What do you mean?' asked Wendy who looked very confused.

'When the king banished me, he said I was to go as far away from Madison as possible. He took me into his

46

map room and told me to pick a map and whichever one I picked is where I'd be sent to. There were hundreds of different maps to choose from. I randomly picked the London map, Gibbons Road to be precise. The king told me there would be a house there for me where I could live and two cats who would keep me safe. He wanted to keep me far away from Madison. There were two guards watching me the whole time in-case I tried to escape.'

Wendy looked cross, 'I hate him for doing that to you James.'

James shrugged, 'There was nothing I could do, he was so angry.'

'How does this chest work?' she asked curiously

'Well, it's only meant to transport one person at a time, not two people and a dog! That was why they got split up and landed in different places.' He stood up. 'How long ago did they leave and where are they going?'

'Not long ago at all,' Wendy told him. 'They're heading to the coast first and then getting a boat to the palace to see the king in the hope of finding Max. If you hurry you should be able to catch them up and get on the boat too! I'll quickly make you some snacks for the journey.'

James smiled with gratitude, 'You are too kind Wendy, thank you so much.'

'Don't blame yourself James. What the king did to you is terribly unfair. Fate has bought you back here for a reason. You must find Madison, she belongs with you, not Logan.'

'You're right Wendy, I can't tell you how much I want to be with her.'

Wendy smiled at him, 'If there's one thing I know it's how much that girl loves you. Now get going!'

She passed James a bag of snacks and took him to his old bike.

'Ahhhh… Wendy.' He looked so pleased. 'You kept my old bike. I've missed this.'

He jumped on and put the snacks in the front basket and pedalled furiously into the jungle.

Wendy waved him goodbye, 'Good luck my darling James.'

Mental Max scaring off Boris and Doris

The magical chest

Izzy and Columbus settling in for their first
night on Nakamomo Island

Izzy flying on Alex's back, on their way to
meet Wendy

James surprising Wendy at her house

WENDY'S DELICIOUS BANANA BREAD

1 STICK OF BUTTER
1 CUP OF COCONUT SUGAR
2 EGGS
3 BANANAS - MASHED & RIPE
2 CUPS OF FLOUR
1/2 A TEA SPOON OF BAKING SODA
1 TEA SPOON VANILLA EXTRACT

BAKE IN THE OVEN FOR 60 MINS UNTIL GOLDEN
ENJOY!

SHHHH DON'T TELL TOO MANY PEOPLE IT'S A SECRET RECIPE!

The gang about to fall asleep under the stars

CHAPTER FIVE

The dangerous canoe trip

Izzy and the gang had been travelling down the river in the canoe for several hours. They were taking it in turns to paddle. Alex decided he wouldn't fly so he perched on the front to keep a look out. They had spotted all kinds of wildlife, stunning birds and groups of spider monkeys in the trees.

Columbus was having a little swim in the river, until Izzy, to her horror, spotted a crocodile!

'Columbus! Get back into the canoe!' she yelled in a panic.

'Why what's wrong Izz?' he said as he started to slowly paddle back.

'Crocodile Columbus! Get out now!!'

Columbus suddenly caught sight of it, he swam frantically up to the boat but the crocodile had already seen Columbus. It thrashed its huge, shiny tail up in the air and darted towards him with an evil looking snarl.

'Leave him alone you nasty creature!' shouted Izzy.

Columbus finally reached the side of the boat. He looked up to see Alex and Martin eagerly waiting to pull him up. The crocodile approached Columbus's legs with his mouth getting wider and wider. With all their might Alex and Martin got Columbus out of the water just in time. Izzy immediately grabbed him and held him close. The crocodile hissed and disappeared under the murky water.

'Oh Columbus you're shaking you poor thing, I don't know what I'd do if something happened to you.' she said as she stroked his furry, wet face. ' Thanks for helping guys, that was a close call!'

'Yes that was quite scary! Any time Izzy, we're a team and we will always have each other's backs,' said Alex.

Izzy smiled.

'Hear, hear!' said Martin. 'After that drama, I'm feeling a tad peckish!'

Izzy opened up the bag that Wendy had given her and pulled out five fresh coconuts, a loaf of banana bread, and some of Wendy's famous chocolate.

'Yummy.' she said.

Everyone grabbed a coconut.

'How do we open these?' asked Izzy curiously.

'It's very easy, said Martin. 'We just need to crack it open.'

He cracked the coconut onto the side of the canoe and it split in half, he poured the sweet water into his furry mouth. 'Well that certainly hit the spot,' he said licking his lips. Izzy did the same and gave it to Columbus who was calming down and drying off in the sunshine.

They were almost at the coast now. The current was starting to pick up, pulling them along faster and faster.

Izzy started to get a little worried, 'Alex, we're going super-fast now! Are we going to be alright?'

'Don't worry Izzy!' Alex shouted back. 'We're approaching the sea now! Everyone, hold on tight, there are rocks coming up!'

The canoe was picking up more and more speed and wobbling from side to side. Izzy hung on firmly to the side of the canoe and pulled Columbus tightly to her.

'Once we get passed these rocks the water will be much calmer,' Alex reassured them as a huge spray hit him right in the face.

'Yes,' agreed Martin. 'Once we get passed the big waterfall we will be there!'

Izzy looked up in shock. 'What waterfall Alex!?' she shouted looking rather worried pulling Columbus closer to her.

'Don't worry! It will be fun!' yelled Alex as he ruffled his feathers with excitement. 'Just like a ride! We are coming up to the waterfall now! Everyone hold on tight! Martin, put that banana bread away and hold onto the side. You don't want to go fall off do you?'

Martin quickly stuffed the last bit of bread into his mouth and held on.

The canoe approached the huge waterfall, Izzy closed her eyes she was too scared to watch.

'Open your eyes Izzy!' said Martin. 'You're missing the best bit!'

Izzy opened her eyes, she could taste salt in her mouth, all she could see was white… 'We're flying!' she yelled as the water splashed her face. 'This is amazing!'

'Whoooo hoooooo!' screamed Alex. 'I told you it was fun!'

The canoe was falling through the air and then hit the sea with an enormous splash, the whole gang cheered.

'We made it!' Izzy yelled, laughing. 'That was the most exciting ride I've ever been on!'

She took in her surroundings and looked around her, there was a magnificent boat moored up by the beach. Her mouth widened with surprise as she pointed to it. 'Alex is *that* your boat?'

'Oh yes there she is, I've missed her,' Alex replied as they headed towards it.

Martin's eyes came out on stalks, 'Alex, that's not a boat, that's a ship!'

Izzy agreed, 'It's humongous! I never dreamed it would be this big or this magical! How many rooms does it have?'

'Hmmmm… ' Alex paused to think. 'Well, it has ten luxurious bedrooms, you can take your pick. There is also a games room, living room, dining room, a big kitchen fully stocked with all sorts of delicious food. Oh, and then the crew cabins down below.'

'You have a crew?' asked Izzy.

'Of course Izzy, you can't sail a ship this big without a crew. I don't think of them as a crew really, they're more like my friends. Great bunch! Come on, I'll introduce you to them.'

Alex flew off to his ship while the others paddled to the shore.

Martin jumped out first, and then helped Izzy climb onto the sand.

Columbus leapt out last and ran around on the beach.

Alex had gathered his crew on the beach to meet the gang. They all excitedly ran over, Columbus bounded ahead.

They were greeted by four smiley, rosy cheeked chaps

who were all smartly dressed in white sailing outfits.

'Right gang,' said Alex, in an excited tone, 'let me introduce you to my crew. This is Buck my newest member. He is one of the strongest people I know and a great asset to the team.'

Buck was short but stocky with a rather large head. He had muscly arms covered in tattoos.

Buck laughed, 'Hello all, it's a pleasure to have you aboard. I've only been working here for a few months and it already feels like home.'

'Good to hear it Buck,' said Alex. 'How is the repair to the sail coming along?'

Alex explained to the gang that one of the ship's sails had been slightly ripped in a big storm a few days ago.

Buck replied, 'It's almost fixed captain. We will be setting sail in just a few hours.'

'Great stuff! Thank you, Buck. Now then, this younger chap is Buck's little brother, Snook. We call him Snooky.'

Snook was taller than Buck but they had the same friendly face.

'He's been with us for years, he has the most incredible eye sight and can see for miles and miles.'

'Nice of you to say so Alex,' said Snook as he stroked Alex's wing. 'Hello and welcome friends!'

Alex introduced the last two members, 'This is Bugsy

our waiter.'

Bugsy was very pale and had light blonde hair, he was slim with blue eyes.

'He's an incredible story teller. Many nights have been spent on the top deck looking at the stars while Bugsy tells us the most amazing stories.'

Bugsy smiled, 'Welcome friends! Yes, I do love to tell stories - my head is filled with so many fantasy adventures. I could tell you all one tonight after dinner if you like?'

They all nodded their heads and Izzy said, 'Oh yes Bugsy we would love that. It feels like we're on a fantasy adventure of our own!'

They all laughed.

'And, last but not least, this is Chester, our chef!'

Chester was a very large man with curly ginger hair and a big ginger beard.

'He will be cooking you all a big feast tonight!'

Chester shook their hands, 'Great to have you all aboard! Indeed, I hope you're all hungry, I'll be cooking up a storm later!'

Columbus's ears pricked up and Martin licked his lips.

'We are famished,' said Martin as if he hadn't eaten for days. 'I couldn't be more excited for dinner followed by a great story. Thank you all for being so hospitable.'

They all climbed a rope ladder onto Alex's ship. Alex showed them to their cabins. Each room was beautifully decorated.

Alex showed Izzy and Columbus into a particularly large cabin, 'I think you'll like this one,' he said, opening a door to reveal the most incredible bedroom with a huge four-poster bed. It was the biggest bed they'd ever seen and had sheets of gold silk and big fluffy pillows.

'Alex, this bedroom is awesome!' said Izzy running over to the window. 'Look Columbus, you can see the ocean for miles!'

Columbus sniffed around the room and then jumped up on the bed and rubbed his furry head on the sheets, 'It's so soft, thanks Alex!'

Alex smiled, 'You're both very welcome. Now get settled in, everything you need will be in your bathroom. Dinner is served in an hour, I'll see you then.'

Columbus and Izzy started jumping up and down on the bed laughing.

'Let's check out the bathroom,' said Izzy jumping off.

The bathroom was huge, it was sparkling white with dark wood.

'I'm going to have a lovely hot bath,' Izzy announced running the bath and pouring in lots bath foam.

'While you're having a lovely bubble bath, I'm going to have a little nap. Wake me up in time for dinner please.'

'Of course I will Columbus, we wouldn't want you missing that.'

Izzy ran her bath, even though she was so grateful to be on Alex's ship she couldn't not stop thinking about Max and how he should be there too. She prayed he was safe and hoped the king would know where he was.

CHAPTER SIX

Chester's big feast

After the gang had settled in they all headed upstairs to the main dining area where they were greeted by Bugsy, 'Hello friends! I hope you are all very hungry, Chester has been cooking something special for you all.'

Bugsy showed them to the dining room where the crew spent most of their time. It was quite an old fashioned room bursting with stories with a dart board on the wall and a big map of the Island. The room was lit by a large antique lamp hanging from the ceiling which gave it a really cosy feel.

'This is great!' Martin exclaimed as he jumped up and wrapped his tail around the hanging lamp.

Suddenly a very hot and sweaty Chester burst through the doors, 'Hello everyone, dinner is almost ready.'

They all cheered.

'On tonight's menu we will be starting with a seaweed and oyster soup followed by slow roasted hog's tail, one each, served with all the trimmings. To finish off I've made my famous passion fruit and lychee tart with vanil-la-pod cream.'

The gang were very impressed, particularly Columbus who was almost dribbling. Martin looked at Izzy. 'Have you tried pig's tail before? It's a speciality in the jungle.'

'I've tried pork but never a pig's tail,' giggled Izzy, 'I'm excited to try something new, I'm sure I'll love it.'

Buck and Snooky then came in, 'Hello everyone!' they greeted, as they both sat down at the table, 'Chester, what's on the menu tonight?'

'Too late guys,' Chester replied, in a grumpy tone. 'You've missed the announcement. I'm not repeating myself again.' He turned around in a huff and headed back into the kitchen.

The crew all laughed including Alex.

'Chester likes us all to be on time for dinner,' said Buck smiling.

Snook, who was still giggling, added, 'He takes it very seriously. Now we may be late for dinner but we have good news! The sail is all fixed so can we set sail shortly!'

'Nice work boys!' Alex congratulated flapping his wings, 'I'm just going to pop to the upper deck to check it all out. I'll be back soon before Chester notices.'

While they were waiting for dinner, Izzy told the guys all about their adventure so far, about Max and why they were on their way to see the king. The guys couldn't believe it - they were fascinated by her story. As they were asking Izzy lots of questions about London, Alex returned, 'Izzy, look who has found us... '

Izzy immediately stood up thinking it was Max. Then, to her amazement, a very exhausted Mr. Niri walked in....

Izzy was in total shock, he was the last person she expected to see. He looked so different, he had more colour in his face and a sparkle in his blue eyes.

'Mr Niri!' she cried, as the whole table gasped. 'How ever did you find us here?'

'Hi Izzy I'm so glad I've found you all. Please, call me James. After you travelled here, through my magical chest, I came looking for you,' a very out of breath James explained, 'I stopped by to visit my old friend Wendy and she told me everything that had happened. I've been cycling like crazy to catch you up.'

Alex showed James to the table. 'Please sit down James, rest and join us for dinner.'

'Thank you, Alex,' James said, sitting down with a sigh of relief.

He introduced himself to everyone at the table.

Izzy was bursting with a million questions she wanted to ask him, 'James, do you know where Max is?'

'No. I'm sorry Izzy, I don't know where he could be. My chest is only meant to transport one person at a time, which is why you got split up.'

'You shouldn't be sorry, I'm the sorry one,' said Izzy with her head in her hands, 'I feel so terrible about breaking into your house Mr Niri. Oh sorry, James. I need to get used to that. Anyway, Columbus's ball went flying through your open window and I was too scared to ask for it back so we decided to just go in and get it.'

James looked confused, 'Of course I would have given it back, why were you so scared to ask me?'

Izzy nervously dipped her head to the ground, 'I don't quite know how to say this… we thought you were… a, a… vampire.'

James burst out laughing, 'A vampire! Why would you think that!?'

Izzy started laughing too, 'I know it's so silly. One of our neighbours said she saw you drinking blood once.'

'That wasn't blood!' said James who was finding this all very amusing. 'That was tomato juice, I'm always drinking it.'

They both laughed together and Izzy felt very foolish for ever believing Maisie McKelling's stupid story. She couldn't wait to tell Max how wrong they'd been about Mr Niri.

After James had finishing laughing at the ridiculous mix up his face grew more serious, 'Wendy told me you're all heading to see the king. I guess he's your best bet at finding out where Max is. I'll come with you, but the king cannot find out that I'm here.'

'I hope he'll know where Max is, I'm so worried about him James, I just want to know he's safe!' Izzy went on to explain that she knew all about what had happened with Madison and told him how unfair she thought it all was. James smiled gratefully, thanking them all for being so kind and welcoming.

Alex smiled at James, 'Pleasure! After dinner Bugsy will show you to one of our cabins. Chester, my wonderful chef, has cooked us all a fabulous dinner. I'll just let him know there will be one extra person at the table - he gets funny about things like that.'

Dinner began, Bugsy brought out the seaweed and oyster soup, which everyone loved, followed by the main course of slow roasted hog's tails.

'Columbus you look like you're in doggy heaven!' Izzy laughed.

'That was glorious Chester,' said Martin, as he started licking his plate clean.

Chester looked extremely pleased, 'Good stuff, glad you all liked it. Make sure you all have room for my dessert!'

'Oh yes,' Izzy promised. 'I always have room for dessert.'

'That was one of the best meals I've ever had,' James said to Chester.

After they had all stuffed their faces with the passion fruit and lychee tart, Alex asked Bugsy if he could tell everyone one of his lovely stories. Bugsy happily agreed and they all headed up to the top deck. The sky was clear and the stars were brightly shining. The calming sound of the waves and the gentle rocking of the ship made everyone feel incredibly relaxed. Buck and Snooky gave everyone blankets.

'This is glorious,' Martin said, as he threw the blanket around his fury body.

Everyone snuggled up with their blankets and waited for Bugsy to begin. He told them the most wonderful story which all took place in the ocean. It was about a family of fish searching for a new home. He described the scenery with such detail that the whole gang were lost in the magical underwater world he had created. Bugsy finished his story with the most delightful ending - the family of fish had found their new home after meeting lots of new fun characters along the way. It reminded Izzy of the adventure she was on and she started to miss her family.

'That was an excellent story Bugsy,' said Alex as he stretched out his wings.

Izzy agreed with a slightly sad look on her face. 'Yes Bugsy, a brilliant story!'

'What's wrong Izzy?' James asked.

'The story really made me miss my family. I've been so caught up with trying to find Max, I haven't thought about them. I've been missing for a few days now, they must be so worried about me.'

James smiled at Izzy. 'Oh, Izzy I should have told you earlier, when you come here, no time passes back at home. This is Nakamomo Island, it's a very magical and special place. When you go home it will be like you never left. So please don't worry, your family will never know you've been missing.'

Everyone in the group looked gobsmacked.

'So, my family don't even know I've gone? That's crazy!' Izzy exclaimed in shock. 'I knew this place was special but I didn't realize just how magical it was! I'm so relieved they won't be worried about me!'

It had been a long day and it was time to get to bed. They all made their way to their cabins and said good night.

Izzy gave James a hug goodnight, 'I'm so sorry this has happened, I was the one who broke into your house. I should never have done that. Now Max is gone and you will get in trouble with the king for being here, it's all my fault.'

James gave Izzy a reassuring smile. 'I'm so glad you did break in. I'm happy to be back here. I've been so dreadfully unhappy it's about time I did something about it. We will find Max and I'm going to confront the king and get Madison back!'

Izzy jumped up, 'Oh James that's so great! She loves you and you should never have been separated.'

'Thank you Izzy,' said James, with a tear in his eye. 'That's so kind of you. Now, you go and get some sleep, something tells me tomorrow is going to be a big day.'

CHAPTER SEVEN

Tricking Ted and Fred

The sunlight was pouring through the cabin window when Izzy woke up. She looked at Columbus curled up on the end of her bed. She gave him a stroke and he slowly opened his eyes and stretched out his arms with a big yawn.

'Morning Columby bum,' she said, as she wrapped her arms around him and gave him a huge hug.

He licked her face. 'Morning my Izzy Wizz. How did you sleep?'

Izzy had not slept well at all. She couldn't stop worrying about Max and kept imagining he was trapped somewhere awful and there was nothing she could do to help. 'Not great, I just miss Max so much. I really hope we find him.'

'I know Izzy, I miss him too. Max is tough, remember that time when I was a puppy and I got stuck in the river and couldn't get out? You were crying and couldn't reach me. Max jumped in instantly and pulled me out. He ruined his brand-new watch that he'd got for his birthday but that didn't bother him. All he cared about was that I was safe.'

Izzy wiped away her tears with a smile. 'Oh yes I remember! He was so brave. You're right, if anyone can survive alone on a strange island, it's Max.'

They could hear the others starting to wake up and then they heard Chester announce breakfast was served.

Columbus's ears shot up and he ran to the door, 'Come on Izzy, let's go!'

'I just need to get ready first Columbus. I'll meet you up there.' She'd barely finished her sentence before he ran out the door.

When Izzy was ready, she headed upstairs to the dining room for breakfast.

'Morning Miss Izzy,' said Bugsy, as he pulled up a chair for her.

'Good morning Bugsy,' said Izzy. 'Morning everyone.'

Chester burst through the doors. 'Morning Izzy! I asked Columbus last night what you'd like for breakfast and he told me all about the Full English Breakfast. I admit I've not heard of this before, so I checked all my recipe books and finally found it. It was in an old book right at the back of the shelf. Fascinating recipes. I'm going to try and cook a Sunday Roast next!'

Izzy laughed. 'That's so cool Chester! I bet your Sunday Roast would be the best. So, you've cooked a Full English Breakfast? I can't wait to see this!'

Chester grinned from ear to ear and asked Bugsy to start bringing out the breakfast. There were eggs, bacon, sausages, baked beans, mushrooms, tomatoes, and a big pile of toast.

'Isn't this great Izzy!' said James, helping himself to some sausages.

'Wow, this is the coolest breakfast ever!' said Izzy. 'All my favourite things. This will definitely set us up for our big day today. Good work Chester!'

Everyone else was busy stuffing their faces. Martin had never had an English breakfast before. His little furry chin was covered in tomato sauce and he was going in for seconds and thirds. When everyone had finished, Buck and Snooky came in yelling they were only an hour away from the palace.

Everyone cheered.

'Yes!' said Izzy. 'I might finally get to see Max! Right

guys, how do we get to the king?'

James explained, 'He has two main guards called Ted and Fred. They are not the smartest of chaps but very picky about who they let in. I'll have to disguise myself so they don't recognise me.'

'How are you going to disguise yourself?' asked Izzy.

'Oh, I have an idea,' Alex shouted, as he ruffled his feathers. 'You can wear a black cloak I have. It used to belong to an old crew member. It has a drooping hood that can hide your face.'

'Thanks Alex, that might just work,' James agreed, looking slightly nervous.

'What do you think will happen if they recognise you?' asked Izzy.

'Well, the king has banished me and told me to never return so I imagine he'll be extremely angry. Who knows what he'll do. He is not a nice man.'

Izzy sighed. 'Let's just hope that we can get you past the guards, then the rest is down to you.'

'I can see the palace ahead!' Snooky shouted.

The palace was located on Nakamomo Island's most beautiful coast. It was surrounded by white sand, tall palm trees and wonderfully unique and exotic plants beaming with colour. As the ship grew nearer, the whole gang were crowded on the top deck eager to see more.

The ship pulled into the bay and with a rattling of chains. Buck released the anchor.

'We have arrived folks!' Buck shouted.

Everyone clapped.

'Splendid journey chaps, well done,' grinned Martin.

'I can't believe we're finally here!' said Izzy.

James put on the cloak that Alex had given him. The large hood was big enough to hide most of his face.

'Can you tell it's me?' he asked the gang, as he turned around.

'Not at all,' Izzy replied. 'You look like a wizard.'

They all decided to pretend that he was a local wizard that had helped Izzy get to the palace.

'Good idea,' said James, looking less terrified.

Izzy turned to Buck, Snooky, Bugsy, and Chester, 'You have all been so lovely and welcoming. Chester, your cooking has been fantastic! Bugsy, you are the best story teller ever. Buck and Snooky, without you guys we would never have got here. You are all very special. I really hope to see you again.'

They all gave Izzy a hug and wished her good luck.

'Alex, are you coming with us?' Izzy asked.

'Are you kidding?' he replied. 'I've come this far, and I want to see you reunited with Max. You just try and stop me!'

Izzy wrapped her arms around Alex's soft and silky body

and gave his beak a kiss. He blushed and flew up in the air with excitement.

'OK everyone, time to go!' Izzy announced, as she marched off the ship, leading them towards the rainforest. They made their way through the jungle until they came up to a deep moat surrounding the palace. There was only one way across - a flimsy rope bridge.

On the other side stood Ted, the king's guard.

They all walked very slowly across the bridge, one by one, with Alex flying above. As they carefully took each step the bridge wobbled and creaked dangerously.

Izzy stared down at menacing jagged rocks below them, 'Is this safe James? It doesn't feel safe,' she said, almost losing her balance.

'Yes, don't worry,' he replied. 'No one has ever fallen, well… not recently anyway.'

They eventually came to the end of the bridge, everyone sighed with relief.

'See, I told you it was safe. There's Ted,' James whispered. 'Izzy, you do the talking.'

Izzy nodded her head and walked towards him. He immediately snapped to attention. 'Welcome to the Nakamomo Kingdom.'

Ted was a rather skinny guard. He was very tall and wore a pointed helmet. 'What are you all doing here?' he asked, trying to see who was under the cloak.

Izzy stepped forward. 'Hello there,' she said nervously. 'We are here to, er... to see the king.'

'The king?' asked Ted suspiciously. 'What about?'

'Well, it's complicated,' Izzy replied. 'You see, I'm from London. I came here with my friend and now he is lost, and I need to ask the king if he knows where he is.'

Ted looked baffled. 'You came from where?!'

'London, England,' stated Izzy.

'And who are these animals?' Ted asked curiously.

'This is my dog, Columbus. And these are my friends who helped me get here, Alex, Martin and a local wizard.'

Ted stared at James. 'Wizard you say. We don't get many wizards around here. Take off your hood, wizard.' he ordered.

James stood still and did nothing.

Izzy panicked and burst out, 'No no no. He is very shy. Look, we mean no harm. We just want to see the king... '

Ted took off his helmet and scratched his head. 'Hmmmm,' he pondered.

James stepped forward angrily. 'Just let us through!' he exploded. 'We have been travelling for days and need to see the king.'

Then something very strange happened. The ground began to shudder and James's cloak started glowing.

Ted looked ahead, mesmerised by the cloak. He seemed to have gone into a trance. 'Yes, you must all go through at once!' he said in a strange voice. His eyes stared blankly as he slowly opened the gate. Everyone looked at each other in shock as they marched through.

'Er thanks,' said a very confused Izzy.

They started walking towards the next gate where they could see Fred, the other guard, eagerly waiting for them.

'What just happened?' Izzy asked, turning to the group.

'It's this cloak,' James exclaimed in astonishment. 'It's magical. I've heard of these cloaks but I've never seen one, let alone worn one!'

'That was amazing!' said Columbus, looking up at James. 'He did exactly what you told him to do!'

'I know, this cloak is powerful. Where did you get it from again, Alex?'

'It belonged to an old crew member called Mevvie. He was a lovely man. There was something very unique about him. I found the cloak in his room after he'd gone. I just assumed it was a standard cloak and put it away. I had no idea it was magical.'

'Sounds like Mevvie might have been a real wizard. Let's see what this cloak can really do!' James suggested excitedly as he hurried towards Fred.

As they all got closer to Fred, they could see he was in the middle of eating a large chocolate bar. He was a fat man, almost bursting out of his smart uniform. His hat was wonky and his hands were covered in melted chocolate. He saw James and the gang approaching, so he quickly finished the chocolate bar and licked his fingers. 'Welcome to the Nakamomo Kingdom,' he said, standing to attention. 'What is your business here?'

James stepped forward. 'We are selling the finest cakes in all the Island; the king requested us to come.'

Fred looked very excited at the idea of the cakes, but he wanted some for himself first. 'The king has not informed me of this. I cannot let you through.' He looked coy. 'I could be persuaded with a little sample of your goods though?'

James smiled cunningly. As he turned away from Fred his cloak shook and suddenly a huge cake appeared. It was four times the size of Fred! It was a magnificent vanilla sponge with a gooey, jam centre.

Fred's eyes were out on stalks. He was almost speechless. 'How did you… what the…' he stammered, gazing up at the delicious treat before him.

'That will keep you going Fred.' James laughed with a smirk as he strode proudly through the gate. 'Come on guys let's go in.'

The gang followed James leaving a very dumfounded Fred behind them. It didn't take Fred long before he was gobbling large chunks of scrumptious cake.

'That was awesome!' Izzy congratulated James, barely containing herself. 'That was one of the coolest things I've ever seen! A giant cake. Genius!'

Everyone was enthralled at what the cloak could do.

'As much fun as that was,' James cautioned, as he began to take it off, 'this cloak could be dangerous.'

'Dangerous? How?' Izzy asked.

Columbus looked puzzled. 'What could be dangerous about being able to do whatever we want?'

James explained that if the cloak fell into the wrong hands it could be very harmful. 'We've had our fun, but now we should hide this. We can figure out later what to do with it.'

They agreed with James and hid the cloak under a large fern.

James turned to Izzy. 'Thanks. Trust me it's better this way. Don't worry, we will find out where Max is immediately,' he promised.

Izzy understood.

They all headed closer to the palace.

'Stunning isn't it,' James sighed looking up at the towers and ramparts. 'You see the tall tower up there? That top window is Madison's room.'

'Beautiful,' Izzy marvelled, looking up. 'Let's find the king. He must know where Max is. James, when we've found him, you have to talk to Madison.'

'Yes, I must,' James agreed, nervously. 'The king has probably just finished his lunch in the grand dining room. Let's head over there now. I know the way, follow me.'

CHAPTER EIGHT

Meeting the king

The gang entered through the palace doors. It was beautifully decorated inside with a white marble floor and stone statues of past kings. Sunlight shone through the huge glass windows and bounced off the pure gold ceiling. There was a large ornamental pond with a fountain in the centre. It was full of tropical fish and the water glistened in the warm rays of the sun. In the corner a lady sat playing a harp. She looked lost in the music as it echoed around the room.

Columbus immediately darted towards the fish until Izzy called him back.

'No Columbus, leave the fish alone, we must be well behaved in here.'

He skidded to a halt and looked sheepish.

'This way,' whispered James, pointing down one of the many hallways.

They all headed further and further into the magnificent palace.

Alex and Martin were dragging behind the others, overwhelmed with how stunning it all was.

'Isn't this great, I've always wanted to know what the palace was like inside,' Alex said quietly to Martin, as he flew around examining every nook and cranny.

'Oh yes, me too,' Martin replied, attempting to contain his excitement. 'And now, here we are, going to meet the king!'

As they all approached the grand dining room they could hear a very loud and deep laugh.

James turned to the gang and whispered, 'I'd know that laugh anywhere. That's him, that's the king.'

Izzy gulped nervously. 'You guys stay here. I'll go in first.'

She walked nervously into the spectacular dining room. Enormous glass doors opened onto beautiful landscaped gardens.

The king was the only one sitting at the head of a long dining table, guzzling wine and eating a large blueberry pie. He was slightly overweight with curly blonde hair and a thick beard, a friendly looking man, but with sadness behind his eyes. There were two guards standing to the side of him gazing out of the window looking extremely bored.

The king saw Izzy walk in. He stared at her for a while.

'You must be the famous Izzy,' he said, wiping blueberry juice from his beard.

The guards suddenly stood to attention.

Izzy looked shocked. 'How do you know my name?' she asked, confused.

'I know all about you,' he said. 'I have eyes and ears all over this island. You're looking for Max, aren't you?'

'Yes!' Izzy burst out. 'Do you know where he is?'

The king ignored her question. 'Who did you come here with?'

'I came with my friends,' she answered proudly, beckoning them over. 'This is Columbus, Alex, and Martin. They've been helping me search for Max.'

Martin stepped forward attempting to contain his excitement. 'It is a pleasure to finally meet you, sir.'

The king nodded at him.

'James!' The king called out in a demanding, loud voice. 'You can come in now.'

James walked in awkwardly and stood by Izzy. 'So, you knew I was here?'

'I know everything James,' boasted the king smugly. 'You've got a lot of guts coming back here.'

The king stood up and called out for one of his servants. 'Simmy!' 'Cooommmmming,' Simmy replied, in a very slow manner.

'He's a bit slow,' the king explained. 'He's worked here for years.'

Finally, Simmy appeared. He was a sloth - a small, funny looking furry creature with a smiley face.

'Simmy, my old friend!' greeted James. 'It's great to see you again.'

Simmy slowly crawled into the room and looked up. 'Jaaaames,' he greeted with a slothful smile, his furry eyebrows rising in surprise. 'How lovely to see yooooou here. I've missssssssed yooou.'

The king asked Simmy to bring out a jug of fresh lemonade and then invited them all to follow him out onto the terrace. The sun was beaming down and the birds were chirping. There were comfortable chairs with colourful silk cushions. Columbus ran off searching for sticks.

The king sat down with a sigh of contentment. 'Glorious day isn't it,' he remarked.

Izzy was getting frustrated. 'Yes, it's lovely,' she agreed politely. 'Sorry, but do you actually know where Max is? It's just we've been looking for him for days now, and I'm desperate to know if he's safe!'

The king laughed. 'Oh, he's safe alright.'

'Whatever does that mean?' asked Izzy.

The king smiled knowingly. 'Max is here. He's been

82

staying here ever since one of the guards found him wandering around outside the gates. Quite the cheeky chappie, isn't he?'

Izzy jumped up out of her seat. 'Max is here! Where? I want to see him!'

'He's upstairs in the right wing. Madison has been looking after him. They've become good friends.'

James looked up, 'Madison? So, she is here then?'

The king scrunched up his face at James. 'Yes, she's here, but you are not seeing her.'

Just as James opened his mouth to argue, Simmy lumbered outside with some snacks. He slowly offered sandwiches to the gang.

'Excuuuuuuuuuse me, sir?' he said to the king.

'Yes, Simmy?'

'Can I make a suggeeeeeestion? Seeing as James has come baaaaaaack for Madison, why don't yoooooooou put him through the 'Rings of Fire'? You've been dying to try it ouuuuuuut and James could be the perrrfect candidate… '

The king's face lit up. 'Yes Simmy! Great idea!' he agreed, rubbing his hands together.

'If James faaaaaaaails he must leave forever. But…' Simmy turned slowly and looked at James, 'If he wins, you muuuuuuuust allow him to be with Madison and not evvvvvvvver bother them again.'

The king didn't like the idea of that at all. He hoped

James would fail and he would get his own way, so he agreed.

James smiled at Simmy, wondering what he was in for, but grateful for the opportunity to win back Madison.

The king called for his guards. He instructed them to set up 'The Rings of Fire,' a new game that had been sent to him from his cousin Raffa, the ruler of the Majim Rainforest. Raffa was constantly designing new games and sending them to him. This one was the biggest and most dangerous to date.

'What exactly is 'The Rings of Fire" asked Izzy looking worried.

The king announced with a mischievous grin, 'It's a series of three personal challenges. The first ring of fire is to face your ultimate fear. The second is a test of intelligence. The third is the biggest test of all, a test of true love.'

Izzy gave James a fearful glance. 'Are you sure you want to do this James?'

'If there's a chance to be with Madison again it's worth it. Don't worry Izzy, I must do this,' James insisted.

'I know you must and I'm sure you'll win.' Izzy gave him a hug and then broke away with a determined expression. She couldn't wait any longer to see Max. 'I'm going to get Max, James. Don't do anything until I get back.'

She ran back into the palace and found Simmy in the kitchen. 'Simmy, where can I find Max?'

'Ahhhhhh, Sir Maaaaaaaaax. His rooooooom is

on the third floor, second door on the right. Such a lovely boyyyyyyy.'

'Thanks!' Izzy shouted, heading for the staircase. She ran up to the third floor, banged on the second door to her right and called out; 'Max. Max, it's me, Izzy. Let me in!'

The door flew open. 'Izzy? Izzy! It's you! You're really here!' Max flung his arms around her. 'Where have you been? I've been so worried!'

'Me too Max. I've been worried too. It's been crazy! I'm so relieved I've found you. I have SO much to tell you.'

They sat down on Max's huge bed and Izzy told him everything that had happened.

'And now,' Izzy gasped, almost out of breath, 'James has to do this game called 'The Rings of Fire' to win back Madison. He's down there right now getting ready.'

Max was gobsmacked. He couldn't believe the amazing adventure Izzy had described. 'That's incredible Izzy. Mr Niri is here and he's a nice guy? And what about this posh-talking monkey and toucan? Incredible! But, the most incredible of all is Columbus. I can't believe Columbus can talk. That's awesome!'

'I know! Come on, let's go downstairs. I can't wait for you to meet them!'

Max and Izzy ran downstairs and into the garden where she introduced Martin and Alex to Max. 'Guys, this is Max! I'm so happy you can finally meet!'

Martin greeted Max with a friendly smile, as he held

out his furry arm. 'Hello young Max, we've been on quite an adventure to find you.'

Max, giggling at Martin's posh accent, shook his hand with a huge grin. 'Izzy's told me all about your trip, thanks so much for looking after her.'

Alex flew and perched on Max's shoulder.

'And you must be Alex!?' laughed Max.

'Yep, Sailor Alex. So great to finally meet you. Izzy has told me all about you.'

'I can't thank you guys enough,' Max said gratefully. 'This has been the craziest few days!'

He then spotted Mr Niri and nervously went to shake his hand, 'Hello Mr Niri, I'm Max.'

'Oh please, enough of that. Call me James,' James said, as he gave Max a hug. 'Great to finally meet you.'

Max, who was still getting used to Mr Niri, hugged him back. 'It's nice to meet you too James.' He looked around. 'Izzy, where's Columbus?'

Alex explained that Columbus had gone off searching for sticks.

'Columbus!' Max yelled. 'Where are you buddy?'

Suddenly a very excited Columbus came bounding out from some bushes and darted towards Max. He was very excited to see him. His tail was wagging and his tongue was waving about. He pounced on Max and began licking his face all over.

Max gave him a huge hug. 'I've missed you boy! Izzy

tells me you can talk here? That's amazing!'

'Max! It's so good to see you. We've been so worried. Yep, I can talk here. Can you believe it!'

Before Max could respond, the king was shouting; 'OK enough of that! I want to play my game now! Everyone, follow me. It's time to see if James can beat 'The Rings of Fire."

CHAPTER NINE

The Rings of Fire

Everyone gathered around three huge rings of roaring, bright orange fire. As James stared up at them he felt quite worried about what he had agreed to.

The king saw the look of worry in James's eyes. 'No backing down now James. Time for the first ring!' he proudly announced.

Everyone wished James good luck.

Izzy patted him on the back. 'You can do this James, just think of Madison.' James smiled and began to feel more confident. He thanked the gang and walked towards the first ring.

"The Ring of Fear," the king announced.

Everyone waited for something to happen…

As if by magic, a huge, black, hairy leg covered in brown spikes appeared out of the ring.

Martin gasped. 'What on earth is it?' he shrieked in horror, as another leg appeared, then another, and then a huge body with eight black eyes.

'It's a spider! A humongous spider!' yelled Izzy, as she jumped behind Max.

James was quaking in his shoes.

'Spiders must be his biggest fear,' said Max.

The whole of the spider revealed itself and fastened it's eight black eyes upon James. It's hairy legs moved faster and faster as it furiously began to spin a web getting closer and closer to James.

'James, it's going to trap you in it's web, do something!' shouted Max.

James couldn't move he was so petrified.

The king laughed. 'Try getting out of this one James!' he chortled, rubbing his hands together.

Izzy couldn't stand seeing James so terrified. She desperately tried to think of anything she could do to help. Suddenly she had an idea. 'Be back in a sec!' she told Max, and frantically ran off.

'Where are you going Izz!?' Max yelled.

'I have plan!' she shouted back.

Izzy remembered where they had hidden the cloak

beneath the fern. She grabbed it and hurried back as fast as she could with the cloak clutched in her hands.

As she approached James and the spider, she yelled out to him.

James turned around and Izzy threw him the cloak.

'The only way to fight magic is with more magic!' she cried, as James caught the cloak.

The king did not like this interruption one bit. He sensed that somehow the tables were about to be turned on him.

'Brilliant Izzy!' James cried, as he quickly put on the cloak.

At that moment he vanished!

Everyone gasped in amazement.

A few seconds later he re-appeared standing on top of the spider!

The spider was taken by surprise. Before it could react, James had drawn a huge sword from beneath the cloak.

The gang cheered him on. 'Go James!' they all cried out.

The king was now extremely angry. This was not what he had in mind at all. And then, to anger him even more, James plunged the sword into the gigantic spider's head!

'Yes James!' yelled Max who was jumping up and down.

The spider let out a piercing squeal as black slime oozed out of it's head. It started to slowly crumple to the ground. The ring of fire faded and eventually went out.

James flew down and landed next to the king. 'One ring down, two to go,' he said, with a smug grin.

The king was outraged, his face turning a shocking red colour, as he tore the cloak off James. 'You think you're funny, do you?! Let's see how you cope on the next two rings without your magical cloak!'

James laughed, it was amusing to him to see the king so worked up.

The king announced the next ring, 'The Ring of Intelligence! No one is allowed to give James anything!'

Everyone eagerly waited to see what would happen next.

'I wonder what it will be,' Alex whispered to Martin.

'I have no idea, but this is spectacular entertainment,' replied Martin with his eyes fixed on the ring. Suddenly lots of large black and white squares appeared on the grass beside them.

'What's happening?' asked Columbus, with a puzzled look on his furry face.

'I think I know what this is!' Izzy burst out, with an excited smile as all the squares came together.

'Izzy, it's a chess board!' Columbus cried. 'Your favourite game!'

A small wooden horse appeared, followed by a mini castle...

'It sure is.' Izzy responded. 'I wonder if James knows how to play... '

'He looks very worried, so I think not.' added Max. 'He can't be as good as you. You're unbeatable Izz!'

Izzy smiled, 'Thanks Max. Oh, how annoying that I

can't help him!'

Alex overheard them and flew onto Izzy's shoulder. 'Maybe you can help him, without the king knowing,' he suggested with a wink and lowered his voice. 'If you tell me what move James should make, I'll fly by and whisper it in his ear.'

'It's worth a shot!' Izzy agreed.

By now the whole game had been assembled. All the chess pieces were in the starting position.

James looked panic-stricken. It was time for his first move.

After staring at all his pieces, he slowly pushed one of the pawns forward. He looked over to the other side waiting for something to happen.

The horse piece jumped forward.

'Right,' Izzy whispered to Alex. 'Tell him to move his bishop three squares.'

Alex nodded, and as he causally flew past James, he passed on Izzy's instructions very quietly. James heard them clearly and looked over at Izzy who had a cheeky grin on her face. He smiled back at her, nodded, and then moved his bishop.

'Yes!' said Izzy to herself as her plan was working. She continued to tell Alex to relay her instructions to James who followed them with spectacular success.

The king was starting to get very annoyed at Alex who was flying all over the place. 'Can someone tell that bird to stop that. He's distracting me from the game!'

'He's just spreading his wings,' said Max.

The king looked at him angrily, but before he could reply a loud ringing sound came from the chess board.

'Check mate!' yelled Izzy. 'James has won!'

The gang cheered.

James ran over to Izzy and Alex. 'Thanks for your support guys!' He turned to Izzy and whispered, 'Izzy you're one hell of a chess player. I can't believe the king didn't realise.'

The king was furious that James had won both games so far. He hated not getting his own way. As he stood up to announce the third ring, a voice came from behind him, 'Father? What's going on?'

It was Madison.

Madison had heard the commotion from the game in her room. She was a lovely young woman with long blonde hair and beautiful blue eyes, rosy cheeks and pink lips.

Before the king could answer, she saw James. She gasped and frantically ran over to him. 'My darling James, what are you doing here?' she cried, as tears ran down her cheeks.

James was so overwhelmed to see her, he explained everything that had happened so far. 'And now I am on the third ring. If I win, your father has promised he won't keep us apart anymore. We can finally be together.'

Madison was so excited to hear that and turned to the king. 'Father is this true? Will you really let us be together?'

'Yes, it's true Maddy,' the king replied with a bitter tone and a wicked gleam in his eye. 'But the game is not over yet. There is still one more ring to go! The Ring of True Love.'

'Bring it on,' said James, smiling bravely at Madison.

Everyone gathered around the third ring. The fire was roaring, creating a beautiful orange glow. They waited for something to happen…

Suddenly, there was a loud ringing sound, and the fire around the ring turned bright red.

'What's happening?' Madison cried in alarm, turning to her father.

'I don't know. Why hasn't it started!?' he replied, stamping his feet and getting angrier by the minute.

'Look!' Izzy shouted, pointing to inside the ring, 'It's James and Madison!'

Everyone stared at the ring. There was a glowing image of James and Madison, holding hands while walking through a gorgeous flower garden surrounded by orchids.

Madison gasped. 'James it's us! But, I don't understand… What is the test?'

'Don't you get it,' Izzy grinned. 'It's the test of true love and you've already passed! I think everything that James has done has proved how much he loves Madison. '

The ringing stopped and the fire died down.

Madison congratulated James. 'You've passed all three rings!'

She leapt into the air with happiness.

The king was beside himself with rage. He picked up his chair and threw it at a tree where it splintered into matchwood. Luckily, Simmy managed to calm him down by giving him a glass of lemonade and one of his favourite cakes.

'The ring of Fiiiiiirrrreee has spoken,' Simmie said to him. 'And you muuuuuust now honour your promise.'

The king soon began to see sense and let go of his childish anger. He called James and Madison over and promised he would not stand in their way anymore.

He shook James by the hand. 'You have proven yourself worthy of my daughter's love. You have my blessing, you should be together.'

They were overwhelmed with happiness. Madison flung her arms around James. It was as if she'd awoken from a horrible spell. The whole gang cheered and congratulated them both.

'I'm so pleased for you guys!' Izzy cried out.

Madison looked at Izzy with a welcoming smile. 'Hello, and who might you be?'

'My name is Izzy. It's so nice to finally meet you. James has told me so much about you.'

James laughed. 'Let's go inside Maddie and get some tea, it's a long story.' They both walked off hand in hand.

Izzy jumped up and punched the air. 'Yes!'

Everyone laughed and clapped.

Columbus escaping from the crocodile!

Alex's ship

The Nakamomo
Bounty

The gang excited to enjoy Chester's big feast

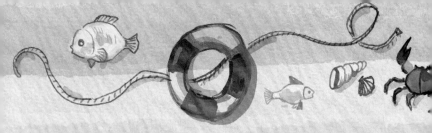

CHESTER'S MENU

Starter

Seaweed and oyster soup

Main

Slow toasted hog's tail served with elephant foot yams, egg plant and black forest pepper with a fig sauce.

Dessert

Passion fruit and lychee tart with vanilla pod and coconut cream

James using the magical cloak to trick Fred

Izzy finally meeting the king!

James playing The Rings of Fire and
killing the giant spider!

Coming up – the amazing jungle party!

Time to say goodbye...

CHAPTER TEN

The jungle party

There was so much to celebrate. Max had finally been reunited with Izzy. Madison and James were together again and more in love than ever.

Because everyone was in such high spirits, the king had decided to throw a huge party at the palace that night and had invited the whole town. All the king's staff had been assigned different jobs to help prepare for the big event.

The party was to be held in the jungle quarters by the palace, with beautiful tree houses connected by rope bridges above cool refreshing rock pools.

As the sun began to set behind the palace, the staff decorated the jungle. They strung up miles of little fairy lights through the branches of the trees and hung up bunches of brightly coloured balloons. The king had arranged for a local steel band to play so they created a big stage by one of the rock pools.

Madison invited Izzy to get ready in her room.

Madison's room was stunning. It was every girl's dream bedroom. A beautiful diamond chandelier sparkled over a gigantic, light pink bed and a gorgeous wooden dressing table with a huge mirror.

'Now, Izzy, let's try and find a dress that's as pretty as you are,' suggested Madison, as she entered a huge walk-in wardrobe full of all her shoes and dresses.

'Wow! Madison, your room is incredible! This walk-in wardrobe is bigger than my bedroom back home,' Izzy laughed. 'Your dresses all look beautiful, but I doubt they will fit me.'

'I still have lots of dresses in your size that I wore when I was your age. My mother gave them to me before she left us and I can't bring myself to get rid of them as they all remind me of her.'

'Oh, I'm sorry to hear that. Do you know where she is now?'

'She's living on another island but she won't tell us which one. My father and mother were never really in love, it was an arranged marriage. I remember them arguing a lot. One day she came into my room, sat me down on my bed and told me she had to go away for a while. I begged her not to. That was seven years ago and she still hasn't returned.'

'That's so sad, Madison,' Izzy said as she gave her a hug .

Madison wiped away a few tears and pulled out four lovely dresses and told Izzy she could take her pick.

'Oh, they're such fabulous colours,' Izzy burst out excitedly, as she felt the fabric of a deep pink dress. There was another electric blue one, an emerald green one and the forth one was crimson. They were all very different and Izzy adored them all. Madison suggested the green one, as it matched her big, green eyes.

Izzy tried it on and it fitted her perfectly. 'Thank you so much, I absolutely adore this.'

At last it was time for the party. The food had been laid out, the fairy lights were all on, and the band had arrived.

'This is going to be a fantastic party!' the king proclaimed, watching a group of bright pink flamingos enter, all wearing shades, carrying surfboards and steel drums.

'King dude!' said one of the flamingos. 'Sorry we're late man, we just got in one last surf of the day, it was rad! We're pumped up and ready to rock.'

'No worries, T-bone,' said the king, showing them over to the stage.

Max looked at Izzy with an excited smile. 'A flamingo band, Izzy! Wicked!'

Izzy laughed. 'Just when I thought I'd seen everything!'

'Open the gates!' the king commanded.

Ted and Fred opened the gates. The townsfolk, cheering with joy, swarmed into the palace. The flamingo band began to play as the king welcomed his guests inside.

Everyone was having a fantastic time. Izzy and the gang were all dancing, well, except for Martin and Alex, who were stuffing their faces with banana bread. The band let them all have a go on the drums - they were having an absolute blast.

'I don't want to leave, Max,' Izzy said, with sadness in her eyes as she danced with him.

'I don't want to go either, Izzy,' Max answered. 'I love it here.'

'Yes, but we have to get back home to our families, I'm really starting to miss them,' Izzy said. 'We need to talk to James about getting home.'

James was on the dance floor with Madison, twirling her around. Izzy went over to him and tapped him on the shoulder.

'Sorry, James, can I steal you away for a moment. Max and I need to talk to you about something important.'

'Of course you can Izzy.' he agreed, suggesting they go inside to escape the loud music.

They all sat down in the drawing room.

'I think I know what you're going to ask,' James began.

'You need to get home now, don't you?'

Izzy nodded. 'We love it here so much. Part of me doesn't want to leave. But now I've found Max, we should really be getting back.'

James completely understood. He explained that there was another magical chest in the palace. He jumped up excitedly. 'Come on, I'll show you the map room.'

Izzy and Max followed James into the king's library. It was a huge and spectacular room, filled floor to ceiling with different kinds of books.

'Cool!' exclaimed Max. 'I've never seen so many books!'

Izzy couldn't believe it, she loved reading. 'This is awesome. Too many books to read.'

James showed them to the back of the room. 'This looks like a normal bookshelf, right?' he said to them.

They both nodded.

'Well, look at this… '

He pulled back one of the books.

Suddenly the bookshelves shook and slid to one side, revealing a secret room.

Izzy's eyes grew wider and wider. 'That's so cool James.'

'This is the map room guys,' James said, as he showed them into a room that looked like it was hundreds of years old. The room was almost cave like with no windows. James lit a candle and hundreds of gem stones twinkled on the ceiling revealing a magnificent chest surrounded by hundreds of maps. The chest looked exactly like the one James had at his house but bigger.

'This is where the king keeps all his special maps,' James told them. 'If you jump into the chest holding one of these maps, that's where you will go.'

Four huge maps were hung up and displayed upon one wall. One of them said *Nakamomo Island*. Izzy curiously went over to the wall to see what the other maps were.

'Oh yes, *The Four Islands*,' said James, as he drew the candle closer to the maps so they could see better. 'These are the main islands here. There's *Nakamomo*, which we are on now, then *Tramaninka*, *Mosikono*, and the biggest of all *Wazunoonoo*.'

Izzy and Max were quite overwhelmed at the thought of more magical islands like Nakamomo.

'Have you been to all of them, James?' Max asked.

'All except Wazunoonoo. The king warned us that it wasn't safe there.'

Izzy looked intrigued. 'Do you know why?' she asked.

'You sure ask a lot of questions you guys,' he grinned. 'There's a king there called Mosaffia. He's an extremely evil and dangerous man.'

Just as Izzy was about to ask more questions, James suddenly said, 'We need to find the right map for London. There must be one with Gibbons Road on it.'

He began searching through stacks of maps, all different sizes and colours until he found what he was searching for.

'Found it!' he shouted proudly.

It was the map they were looking for. *Gibbons Road* was clearly marked, and Izzy could even make out her house.

'Don't we need three of these maps?' she asked.

'Oh yeah,' said Max. 'We don't want to get split up again!'

James laughed. 'Don't worry guys, that won't happen. This chest is a much better and larger version of mine. One map will be fine.'

'Well that's a relief!' Max said, smiling at Izzy.

They headed back to the party to find the others. Izzy had the map firmly grasped in her hand.

The party was beginning to die down and the townsfolk were starting to leave. Izzy and Max agreed they would wait until everyone had left before saying their goodbyes. Alex and Martin had eaten too much and were snoozing under a palm tree. Columbus was hanging out with the flamingo band, they were teaching him how to play the steel drums, while James and Madison were lying in a hammock gazing up at the stars. It was a beautiful night.

'We'd better tell Columbus it's time to leave,' Izzy suggested tearfully.

'Yep, I guess so,' agreed Max, sighing heavily.

Max gathered everyone together under the big palm tree. 'Guys, Izzy and I need to tell you something important.'

Before Max and Izzy had time to speak, Martin woke up and confided in a sad tone, 'We already know what you're going to say.'

'Yes, we knew this moment would come,' Alex said, as he snuggled up to Columbus. 'We don't want you to leave us...'

Max explained that they needed to go home to see their families while Izzy's eyes filled up with tears.

'We will never forget this incredible place,' she told them. 'We've met friends for life here and what an adventure we've all had!'

The king, who also looked like he was about to cry, gave Izzy and Max a hug. 'You are both welcome here any time you like to visit. All you have to do is jump inside James's magic chest again.'

'Thank you so much.' Izzy replied. 'I'm so pleased you and James have put the past behind you.'

'Life is too short,' the king agreed, turning to James and Madison. 'What will you both do now? Do you want to go back with Izzy or will you be staying here?'

James explained to him that he had recognised where the flower garden was from the image that had appeared inside the ring of fire. It was on the other side of the island and they had decided to move there.

'That's a great idea,' said Izzy. 'New beginnings.'

The king agreed as he saw how happy Madison was.

Izzy went and sat next to Martin and Alex who were

both resting their heads on Columbus. 'This is the hardest goodbye of all,' she confessed. 'You've both been amazing. Martin you have a heart of gold. You've made me laugh so much and whenever I see banana bread I'll think of you. Alex, you've gone out of your way to help me find Max. Your ship and crew are just awesome and so cool! You are both lovely friends, I don't know what I would have done without your help.'

By this point everyone was getting very emotional.

'When will you come back to see us?' asked Martin, who had tears rolling down his furry cheeks.

'I have to go back to school in a few days, but I'll come back at half term. I promise.'

'I promise too!' Max said.

'I think it's time to be going now,' said Izzy turning to James to show the way.

'Follow me guys,' said James.

Izzy, Max, and Columbus followed James into the palace. They all felt very sad to be leaving an amazing world and a special group of friends. James took them back into the library, opened up the secret room, and headed over to the chest.

'Time to go now,' Izzy announced, holding up the map. 'James, it will be so weird without you living on our street anymore!'

James laughed. 'I thought you guys were scared of me.'

Max looked embarrassed. 'Well, I was, a bit, but not now! I'll miss you.'

James gave them a kind smile. 'Thank you, Max. I'll miss you both too, but you know you can come back any time to see us all. I think you should both spend time with your families and concentrate on school. That is your world, not this one. It's important you remember that. I'll be back from time to time too.'

He looked at Izzy. 'Izzy, can I ask you a favour?'

'Anything!' Izzy replied.

'Can you feed Boris and Doris for me?'

'Of course, James. I'll take care of them for you.'

She patted Columbus. 'Oh, I just realised, Columbus, you won't be able to talk when we're home.'

Columbus wagged his tail. 'Well, I've found it very weird being able to talk here. Sometimes I just haven't known what to say, but it's been so much fun talking to everyone, especially you Izzy.'

'Oh, Columbus, yes it's been great.' Izzy gave him a huge squeeze clutching the map tightly in her hand. 'Right guys, let's do this!'

They all climbed inside the chest.

'Right, this is it,' James said, closing the lid of the chest. 'Don't get lost now,' he laughed.

'That's not funny James,' said Max, a little nervous.

'Don't worry, I'm just kidding. You'll both be home in no time, I promise.'

'Bye James!' said Izzy holding on to Columbus.

She held Max's hand. They started falling and falling through complete darkness. Before they knew it, they had landed gently on their bottoms, right in the middle of Gibbons Road!

Luckily it was raining so the street was empty, except for one little girl standing under an umbrella. It was Maisie McKelling, she had seen them fall out of the air and was gazing at them wide eyed.

Izzy, Max, and Columbus scrambled to their feet and looked around.

Izzy immediately spotted Maisie staring at them.

'Hey Maisie!' greeted Izzy, as if nothing unusual had happened and Maisie hadn't just seen the three of them appear out of nowhere.

'Oh, hiya, Maisie. Rubbish weather isn't it?' said Max, casually.

Maisie could hardly speak. She stood there under her umbrella in shock.

Izzy's front door opened and her mum yelled out, 'Izzy, Max, get out of the rain and come inside. I've made hot chocolate for you both.'

'Mum!' shouted Izzy, running inside and leaving a very gobsmacked and puzzled Maisie.

Izzy flung her arms around her mum and kissed her on both cheeks. 'Oh, mum, I've missed you so much!'

'What are you going on about, Izzy? You've only been

outside for a few minutes. Now, come in and warm up by the fire. The hot chocolate is in the kitchen. You're welcome to come in too Max. No chocolate for you Columbus, but I do have some juicy sausages with your name on them!'

Izzy and Max ran to the kitchen.

'It's good to be back,' Izzy said to Max, as they sipped their hot chocolate.

'Mum?' she asked. 'What's that in the oven? It smells like bananas?'

'Oh yes,' answered Izzy's mum, as she opened up the hot oven. 'I thought I'd bake some banana bread. I know I've never made it before but I suddenly started craving it! Fancy some?'

Izzy turned to Max and laughed. 'Yes please!'

The end